Mama Will Be Home Soon

By Nancy Minchella

Illustrated By Keiko Narahashi

Scholastic Press · New York

LIBRARY OF CONGRESS CATALOGING-IN-PUBLICATION DATA
Minchella, Nancy.
Mama will be home soon / by Nancy Minchella ; illustrated by Keiko Narahashi. -- 1st ed.   p.   cm.
Summary: Lili spends a few days with her grandmother while her mother is
away and thinks she sees her mother's yellow hat everywhere she goes.

ISBN 0-439-38491-5

[1. Separation anxiety—Fiction. 2. Mother and child—Fiction.
3. Grandmothers—Fiction.] I. Narahashi, Keiko, ill. II. Title.
PZ7.M6525   Mam 2003   [Fic]--dc21   2002003775

10 9 8 7 6 5 4 3 2 1   07 06 05 04 03

Printed in Singapore   46
First edition, May 2003
Book design by David Caplan
The text type was set in Poppl-Pontifex.

To Mary and Gina
who inspired me

and especially to Michael
with love . . .

–n.m.

*L*ili's Mama is going away.

"When are you coming back, Mama?" asks Lili.

"Very soon. I'll be gone just a few days."

"How will I find you?"

Mama squeezes Lili's hand. "You'll see my yellow hat."

Grandma says, "It's time for Mama to go."
Lili holds tight to keep Mama's hug around her.
"Grandma will take good care of you until I come
home. I'll be home very soon." Mama kisses Lili good-bye.
"I love you, Lili."

Mama boards the ferry and waves to Lili. A loud
whistle blows and the ferry pulls away. Lili waves until
Mama's hat is just a speck of yellow, like a flower petal.

Lili holds Grandma's hand as they walk home.
"When is Mama coming home?" Lili asks.
"Soon, Lili, very soon."

In the morning, Lili looks for Mama from her window. She sees something yellow in the yard. "Mama's home!" she shouts and runs outside.

But it is only her sundress drying on the line.

"Mama said she would be home soon, Grandma.
Why isn't she here?"

Grandma holds Lili on her lap. "It's hard to wait, isn't
it? Let's do something special to pass the time."

That afternoon Grandma takes Lili to the circus.
They share candy apples and giggle at the clowns.

Then, Lili sees something yellow.
"There's Mama!" she says.

But it is only a yellow balloon.

"I wish Mama were here," Lili says.
Grandma kisses Lili. "Your Mama wishes
she were here with you, too."

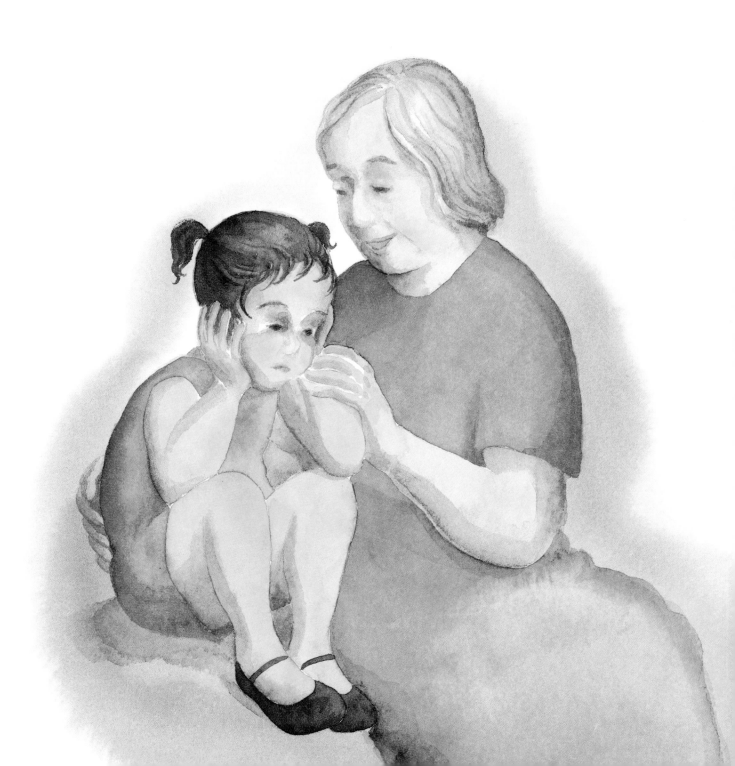

The next day, at the seashore, Lili runs and splashes in the waves. Grandma looks for shells.

Then, Lili sees something yellow.
"I see her, Grandma!"

But it is only a bright yellow umbrella.

Grandma wraps Lili in a warm towel.

"I miss Mama," Lili says.

"I know," says Grandma. She holds a speckled shell to Lili's ear. "Listen, Lili, listen to the sea whisper."

"It sounds sad, Grandma."

"Maybe it's whispering how much Mama misses you."

On their way home through the park, Lili sees something yellow.

"There's Mama!"

But it is only a sunflower.

Lili starts to cry.

"I don't think Mama's ever coming home."

"Oh, but she is!" Grandma says. "She'll be here soon."

"But soon is over and she's not here."

Grandma hugs Lili close. "I know you would like her home today. But it is too soon. We will look for her tomorrow."

"Is tomorrow soon?"

"Yes, Lili, very soon."

Grandma wakes Lili at dawn. "Come, Lili. Soon is almost here. Let's look for Mama."

Grandma and Lili walk through the village to the harbor. "It won't be long now," says Grandma.

The crowd grows bigger. Lili sees specks of yellow everywhere. Yellow skirts, yellow pants, yellow shoes. But no yellow hats. No Mama.

"I don't want to look anymore,"
says Lili. "Mama's never coming."

"Look!" Grandma says. "I see
something yellow."

"It's not Mama. It's probably
a sundress."

Grandma smiles. "No, it's not
a sundress."

"Then it's a balloon or an
umbrella or a sunflower."

"Look!" Grandma says again.
In the crowd, Lili sees a yellow hat.

"Mama!"

Lili runs into Mama's arms and they twirl like a
merry-go-round.

"I found you, Mama! You're home!"

"I'll always come home to you, Lili," says Mama.

Mama reaches in her bag. "I brought you
something, Lili."
"Oh, Mama! My own yellow hat!"

Lili holds Mama tight. She keeps Mama's hug
around her all the way home.